ALADDIN STORY

MR VIVEK KUMAR PANDEY SHAMBHUNATH

Copyright © Mr Vivek Kumar Pandey Shambhunath
All Rights Reserved.

ISBN 979-888569131-4

Disclaimer : During Writing This Book No character & No religious , No Relation Members Are Harmed. It's Only For Study & Entertainment Purpose. Do Not Take Seriously. Short Biopic Written In This Book Written By Mr Vivek Kumar Pandey.

Contents

Foreword

In This Book There Is Aladdin Story In English Languages.During Writing This Book No Character And No Religion Are Harmed. It's Only For Study Purpose. Written By Mr Vivek Kumar Pandey. winner youngest writer award 1st rank in india 2020.He is only one writer can publish 830+ own book that was greatest successfull in his life.This All Credit Goes To My Super Hero Daddy.

Preface

Author biography in English :MY NAME IS VIVEK KUMAR PANDEY . I WAS BORN IN 30 SEP 2002,I AM FROM SURAT GUJARAT INDIA.MY DREAM WAS TO BE GOOD WRITERS ,MY FAMILY SUPPORTED ME TO SUCCESSFUL AND I CAN DO IT MY SELF.How do I write? That is a question, I believe, that can be honestly answered by me."CELEBRATING YOUNGEST WRITER AWARD WINNER IN GUJARAT 1ST RANK" MR PANDEY JI . I may think I did a good job writing something . The reader is the one who decides the quality of my writing. I do find writing to be natural to me and therefore find it to be a real challenge. My trick as a challenged writer is to do the best I can and know that I am happy with the final outcome. It may take a while to do my best and there may be quite a few problems I run into along the way.

I am not a greedy person those who are thinking about me and my self I never tried it anyone people suffering from sadness ,I trying to get promoted people suffering from happiness and joy in your Life Time. Now in current situation in India and also world people are unemployed and have no many but our indian governor help to people to get free food from ration card , i also take part in leadership team ,i am Motivational speaker , Film script writer. There was my two dream firstly writer and secondly actor & also my own film is upcoming soon i done almost completely completed script for my film .I AM GOING TO SAY WORD OF HEART TOUCH OUT PLEASE READ IT" , firstly i thanks my father he supports me in this field they always getting inspired me by own his words and behavior ,they always said that he was a biggest person in the world in future and also they purchase fruit and chocolate for me in anytime & anyway , firstly my father buy him then call me Vivek you want a chocolate i will say yes papa but how many tell me ,papa: you tell me how much i buy him i told 1 or 2 chocolate but my father purchase whole the boxes of chocolate and they get suprised me. MY FATHER WAS BORN IN " 20 SEPTEMBER" 1971 IN INDIA.

1) MY FATHER FAVORITE CLOTHES IS KURTA PAIJMA AND ALSO STYLES SHOE

2) FAVORITE SINGER IS KISHORE DA

3) FAVORITE STATE GUJARAT AND KOLKATA , HIS VILLAGE IN BIHAR

4) FAVORITE COLOR BLACK AND WHITE

THEY ALSO LOVE cricket like IPL and one day t-20 .they also like watching a News daily and heard the song daily ,they also interested in tik tok video but in current time tik tok is banned in india but also few videos are in you tube. In lockdown time my family and me very enjoy day daily. my father play daily ludo with his sister and son, daughter.they always loved tea and coffee anytime call me "। वविके थोडा़ चाय बनाओना वविके तमु्हारे हाथ का चाय अच्छा लगता है". I make it tea for my father but some reason after the April to june they are suffering from fever and cough , weakness on 6 June 2020 my father death. they not told me say bye bye his life. After death of 6 June on 10 june my mom and dad anniversary.but my father is Best in the world they can do anything for me please take care of father and respect it of your parents.

CHAPTER ONE

Ch : 1 Aladdin And The Magic Lamp

Ch : 1 Aladdin And The Magic Lamp

Long time ago in China, there lived a poor boy, whose name was Aladdin. Aladdin lived with his mother. One day a rich and distinguished looking man came to their house and said to Aladdin's mother, "I am a merchant from Arabia and want your son to come with me. I will reward him handsomely." Aladdin's mother instantly agreed. Little did she know that the man pretending to be a rich merchant was in reality a magician.

Next day, Aladdin having packed his belongings left with the 'merchant'. After many hours of traveling the 'merchant' stopped. Aladdin too stopped, surprised that they should stop in such a desolate spot. He looked around; there was nothing in sight for miles.

The 'merchant' pulled out some colored powder from his pocket and threw in the ground. The next instant the whole place was filled with smoke. As the smoke cleared, Aladdin saw a huge opening in the ground; it was a cave. The 'merchant' turned to Aladdin and said, "I want you to go inside this cave; there will be more gold than you have ever seen; take as much as you want. You will also see an old lamp; please bring that back to me. Here, take this ring; it will help you." Aladdin was very suspicious but the decided to do as was told.

He lowered himself into the cave, thinking all the while that it would be difficult to climb out without help. Aladdin entered the cave and just like the 'merchant' had said saw gold, jewelry, diamonds and other valuables. He filled his pockets. When this was done, he looked for the lamp; it was lying in the corner, full of dust and dirty. He picked it up and ran to the cave's opening and shouted to the 'merchant', "I have your lamp. Can you please pull me out?" "Give me the lamp," said the 'merchant'. Aladdin was not sure that he would be pulled out if he gave back the lamp; so he said, "First, please pull me out."

Aladdin and The GenieThis angered the 'merchant'. With a loud cry, he pulled out the same colorful powder and threw it on the cave opening, sealing it with a huge boulder. Aladdin was depressed. He thought, "That was no rich merchant; he was surely a magician. I wonder why this lamp was so important to him." As he was thinking he rubbed the lamp. All of sudden a strange mist filled the room and from the mist emerged a stranger looking man. He said, "My master, I am the genie of the lamp, you have rescued me; what would your wish be?" Aladdin was scared but he said in quivering voice, "Ta.. Take me back home."

And the next moment Aladdin was home hugging his mother. He told her of the magician and the lamp. Aladdin again summoned the genie. This time when the genie appeared he was not scared. He said, "Genie, I want a palace, not an old hut." Again to Aladdin and his mother's amazement in front of them was a magnificent palace.

Time passed. Aladdin married the Sultan's daughter and was very happy. It so happened that the evil magician got to know of Aladdin's good fortune. He came by Aladdin's palace pretending to exchange old lamps for new. The princes, Aladdin's wife, not knowing the value of the lamp to Aladdin called out to the magician to wait.

As soon as the magician saw the lamp he grabbed it from the princess' hand and rubbed it. The genie appeared, "you are my master and your wish is my command," he said to the magician. "Take Aladdin's palace to the great desert faraway from here," ordered the magician.

When Aladdin came home, there was no palace and no princess. He guessed it must be the evil magician who had come to take revenge on him. All was not lost, Aladdin had a ring that the magician had given to him. Aladdin pulled out that ring, rubbed it. Another genie appeared. Aladdin said, "Take me to my princess."

Soon, Aladdin was in Arabia with his princess. He found his lamp lying on a table next to the magician. Before the magician could react, Aladdin jumped for the lamp and got hold of it. As soon as he had the lamp, Aladdin rubbed it.

The genie appeared again and said, "My master, Aladdin, it is indeed good to serve you again. What is it that you wish?" "I want you to send this magician to another world so that he never harms anybody," said Aladdin. Aladdin's wish was carried out; the evil magician disappeared forever.

The genie carried Aladdin, the princes and the palace back to China. He stayed with Aladdin for the rest of his life.

• 3 •

Aladdin Story part - 1

- Aladdin Story part - 1

There once lived, in one of the large and rich cities of China, a tailor, named Mustapha. He was very poor. He could hardly, by his daily labor, maintain himself and his family, which consisted only of his wife and a son.

His son, who was called Aladdin, was a very careless and idle fellow. He was disobedient to his father and story of aladin mother, and would go out early in the morning and stay out all day, playing in the streets and public places with idle children of his own age.

When he was old enough to learn a trade, his father took him into his own shop, and taught him how to use his needle; but all his father's endeavors to keep him to his work were vain, for no sooner was his back turned than he was gone for that day. Mustapha chastised him; but Aladdin was incorrigible, and his father, to his great grief, was forced to abandon him to his idleness, and was so much troubled about him that he fell sick and died in a few months.

Aladdin, who was now no longer restrained by the fear of a father, gave himself entirely over to his idle habits, and was never out of the streets from his companions. This course he followed till he was fifteen years old, without giving his mind to any useful pursuit, or the least reflection on what would become of him. As he was one day playing, according to custom, in the street with his evil associates, a stranger passing by stood to observe him.

This stranger was a sorcerer, known as the African magician, as he had been but two days arrived from Africa, his native country.

The African magician, observing in Aladdin's countenance something which assured him that he was a fit boy for his purpose, inquired his name and history of some of his companions; and when he had learned all he desired to know, went up to him, and taking him aside from his comrades, said, "Child, was not your father called Mustapha the tailor?" "Yes, sir," answered the boy; "but he has been dead a long time."

At these words the African magician threw his arms about Aladdin's neck, and kissed him several times, with tears in his eyes, and said, "I am your uncle. Your worthy father was my own brother. I knew you at first sight; you are so like him." Then he gave Aladdin a handful of small money, saying, "Go, my son, to your mother, give my love to her, and tell her that I will visit her to-morrow, that I may see where my good brother lived so long, and ended his days."

Aladdin ran to his mother, overjoyed at the money his uncle had given him. "Mother," said he, "have I an uncle?" "No, child," replied his mother, "you have no uncle by your father's side or mine." "I am just now come," said Aladdin, "from a man who says he is my uncle and my father's brother.

He cried and kissed me when I told him my father was dead, and gave me money, sending his love to you, and promising to come and pay you a visit, that he may see the house my father lived and died in." "Indeed, child," replied the mother, "your father had no brother, nor have you an uncle."

The next day the magician found Aladdin playing in another part of the town, and embracing him as before, put two pieces of gold into his hand, and said to him, "Carry this, child, to your mother. Tell her that I will come and see her to-night, and bid her get us something for supper; but first show me the house where you live."

Aladdin Story part - 2

- Aladdin Story part - 2

Aladdin showed the African magician the house, and carried the two pieces of gold to his mother, who went out and bought provisions; and, considering she wanted various utensils, borrowed them of her neighbors. She spent the whole day in preparing the supper; and at night, when it was ready, said to her son, "Perhaps the stranger knows not how to find our house; go and bring him, if you meet with him."

Aladdin was just ready to go, when the magician knocked at the door, and came in loaded with wine and all sorts of fruits, which he brought for a dessert. After he had given what he brought into Aladdin's hands, he saluted his mother, and desired her to show him the place where his brother Mustapha used to sit on the sofa; and when she had done so, he fell down and kissed it several times, crying out, with tears in his eyes, "My poor brother! how unhappy am I, not to have come soon enough to give you one last embrace!" Aladdin's mother desired him to sit down in the same place, but he declined.

"No," said he, "I shall not do that; but give me leave to sit opposite to it, that, although I see not the master of a family so dear to me, I may at least behold the place where he used to sit."

When the magician had made choice of a place, and sat down, he began to enter into discourse with Aladdin's mother. "My good sister," said he, "do not be surprised at your never having seen me all the time you have been married to my brother Mustapha of happy memory.

I have been forty years absent from this country, which is my native place, as well as my late brother's; and during that time have travelled into the Indies, Persia, Arabia, Syria, and Egypt, and afterward crossed over into Africa, where I took up my abode. At last, as it is natural for a man, I was desirous to see my native country again, and to embrace my dear brother; and finding I had strength enough to undertake so long a journey, I made the necessary preparations, and set out. Nothing ever afflicted me so much as hearing of my brother's death. But God be praised for all things! It is a comfort for me to find, as it were, my brother in a son who has his most remarkable features."

The African magician, perceiving that the widow wept at the remembrance of her husband, changed the conversation, and turning toward her son, asked him, "What business do you follow? Are you of any trade?"

At this question the youth hung down his head, and was not a little abashed when his mother answered, "Aladdin is an idle fellow. His father, when alive, strove all he could to teach him his trade, but could not succeed; and since his death, notwithstanding all I can say to him, he does nothing but idle away his time in the streets, as you saw him, without considering he is no longer a child; and if you do not make him ashamed of it, I despair of his ever coming to any good. For my part, I am resolved, one of these days, to turn him out of doors, and let him provide for himself."

After these words Aladdin's mother burst into tears; and the magician said, "This is not well, nephew; you must think of helping yourself, and getting your livelihood. There are many sorts of trades. Perhaps you do not like your father's, and would prefer another; I will endeavor to help you. If you have no mind to learn any handicraft, I will take a shop for you, furnish it with all sorts of fine stuffs and linens, and then with the money you make of them you can lay in fresh goods, and live in an honorable way. Tell me freely what you think of my proposal; you shall always find me ready to keep my word."

This plan just suited Aladdin, who hated work. He told the magician he had a greater inclination to that business than to any other, and that he should be much obliged to him for his kindness. "Well, then," said the African magician, "I will carry you with me to-morrow, clothe you as handsomely as the best merchants in the city, and afterward we will open a shop as I mentioned."

The widow, after his promises of kindness to her son, no longer doubted that the magician was her husband's brother. She thanked him for his good intentions; and after having exhorted Aladdin to render himself worthy of his uncle's favor, served up supper, at which they talked of several indifferent matters; and then the magician took his leave and retired.

He came again the next day, as he had promised, and took Aladdin with him to a merchant, who sold all sorts of clothes for different ages and ranks ready made, and a variety of fine stuffs, and bade Aladdin choose those he preferred, which he paid for.

Aladdin Story part - 3

- Aladdin Story part - 3

When Aladdin found himself so handsomely equipped, he returned his uncle thanks, who thus addressed him: "As you are soon to be a merchant, it is proper you should frequent these shops, and be acquainted with them." He then showed him the largest and finest mosques, carried him to the khans or inns where the merchants and travellers lodged, and afterward to the sultan's palace, where he had free access; and at last brought him to his own khan, where, meeting with some merchants he had become acquainted with since his arrival, he gave them a treat, to make them and his pretended nephew acquainted.

This entertainment lasted till night, when Aladdin would have taken leave of his uncle to go home; the magician would not let him go by himself, but conducted him to his mother, who, as soon as she saw him so well dressed, was transported with joy, and bestowed a thousand blessings upon the magician.

Early the next morning, the magician called again for Aladdin, and said he would take him to spend that day in the country, and on the next he would purchase the shop. He then led him out at one of the gates of the city, to some magnificent palaces, to each of which belonged beautiful gardens, into which anybody might enter.

At every building he came to, he asked Aladdin if he did not think it fine; and the youth was ready to answer, when any one presented itself, crying out, "Here is a finer house, uncle, than any we have yet seen." By this artifice the cunning magician led Aladdin some way into the country; and as, he meant to carry him further, to execute his design, he took an opportunity to sit down in one of the gardens, on the brink of a fountain of clear water, which discharged itself by a lion's mouth of bronze into a basin, pretending to be tired. "Come, nephew," said he, "you must be weary, as well as I; let us rest ourselves, and we shall be better able to pursue our walk."

The magician next pulled from his girdle a handkerchief with cakes and fruit, and during this short repast he exhorted his nephew to leave off bad company, and to seek that of wise and prudent men, to improve by their conversation; "for," said he, "you will soon be at man's estate, and you cannot too early begin to imitate their example." When they had eaten as much as they liked, they got up, and pursued their walk through gardens separated from one another only by small ditches, which marked out the limits without interrupting the communication, so great was the confidence the inhabitants reposed in each other. By this means the African magician drew Aladdin insensibly beyond the gardens, and crossed the country till they nearly reached the mountains.

At last they arrived between two mountains of moderate height, and equal size, divided by a narrow valley, which was the place where the magician intended to execute the design that had brought him from Africa to China. "We will go no further now," said he to Aladdin; "I will show you here some extraordinary things, which, when you have seen, you will thank me for; but while I strike a light, gather up all the loose dry sticks you can see, to kindle a fire with."

Aladdin found so many dried sticks that he soon collected a great heap. The magician presently set them on fire; and when they were in a blaze, threw in some incense, pronouncing several magical words which Aladdin did not understand.

He had scarcely done so when the earth opened just before the magician, and discovered a stone with a brass ring fixed in it. Aladdin was so frightened that he would have run away, but the magician caught hold of him, and gave him such a box on the ear that he knocked him down. Aladdin got up trembling, and, with tears in his eyes, said to the magician: "What have I done, uncle, to be treated in this severe manner?" "I am your uncle," answered the magician; "I supply the place of your father, and you ought to make no reply.

But child," added he, softening, "do not be afraid; for I shall not ask anything of you, but that you obey me punctually, if you would reap the advantages which I intend you. Know, then, that under this stone there is hidden a treasure, destined to be yours, and which will make you richer than the greatest monarch in the world. No person but yourself is permitted to lift this stone, or enter the cave; so you must punctually execute what I may command, for it is a matter of great consequence both to you and me."

Aladdin, amazed at all he saw and heard, forgot what was past, and, rising, said: "Well, uncle, what is to be done? Command me, I am ready to obey." "I am overjoyed, child," said the African magician, embracing him. "Take hold of the ring, and lift up that stone." "Indeed, uncle," replied Aladdin, "I am not strong enough; you must help me." "You have no occasion for my assistance," answered the magician; "if I help you, we shall be able to do nothing. Take hold of the ring and lift it up; you will find it will come easily." Aladdin did as the magician bade him, raised the stone with ease, and laid it on one side.

When the stone was pulled up, there appeared a staircase about three or four feet deep, leading to a door. "Descend, my son," said the African magician, "those steps, and open that door. It will lead you into a palace, divided into three great halls. In each of these you will see four large brass cisterns placed on each side, full of gold and silver; but take care you do not meddle with them. Before you enter the first hall, be sure to tuck up your robe, wrap it about you, and then pass through the second into the third without stopping.

Above all things, have a care that you do not touch the walls, so much as with your clothes; for if you do, you will die instantly.

At the end of the third hall, you will find a door which opens into a garden, planted with fine trees loaded with fruit. Walk directly across the garden to a terrace, where you will see a niche before you, and in that niche a lighted lamp. Take the lamp down, and put it out. When you have thrown away the wick and poured out the liquor, put it in your waistband and bring it to me. Do not be afraid that the liquor will spoil your clothes, for it is not oil, and the lamp will be dry as soon as it is thrown out."

After these words the magician drew a ring off his finger, and put it on one of Aladdin's, saying: "It is a talisman against all evil, so long as you obey me. Go, therefore, boldly, and we shall both be rich all our lives."

Aladdin Story part - 4

- Aladdin Story part - 4

Aladdin descended the steps, and, opening the door, found the three halls just as the African magician had described. He went through them with all the precaution the fear of death could inspire, crossed the garden without stopping, took down the lamp from the niche, threw out the wick and the liquor, and, as the magician had desired, put it in his waistband.

But as he came down from the terrace, seeing it was perfectly dry, he stopped in the garden to observe the trees, which were loaded with extraordinary fruit, of different colors on each tree. Some bore fruit entirely white, and some clear and transparent as crystal; some pale red, and others deeper; some green, blue, and purple, and others yellow; in short, there was fruit of all colors. The white were pearls; the clear and transparent, diamonds; the deep red, rubies; the paler, balas rubies; the green, emeralds; the blue, turquoises; the purple, amethysts; and the yellow, topazes. Aladdin, ignorant of their value, would have preferred figs, or grapes, or pomegranates; but as he had his uncle's permission, he resolved to gather some of every sort. Having filled the two new purses his uncle had bought for him with his clothes, he wrapped some up in the skirts of his vest, and crammed his bosom as full as it could hold.

Aladdin, having thus loaded himself with riches of which he knew not the value, returned through the three halls with the utmost precaution, and soon arrived at the mouth of the cave, where the African magician awaited him with the utmost impatience. As soon as Aladdin saw him, he cried out, "Pray, uncle, lend me your hand, to help me out." "Give me the lamp first," replied the magician; "it will be troublesome to you." "Indeed, uncle," answered Aladdin, "I cannot now, but I will as soon as I am up."

The African magician was determined that he would have the lamp before he would help him up; and Aladdin, who had encumbered himself so much with his fruit that he could not well get at it, refused to give it him till he was out of the cave. The African magician, provoked at this obstinate refusal, flew into a passion, threw a little of his incense into the fire, and pronounced two magical words, when the stone which had closed the mouth of the staircase moved into its place, with the earth over it in the same manner as it lay at the arrival of the magician and Aladdin.

This action of the magician plainly revealed to Aladdin that he was no uncle of his, but one who designed him evil. The truth was that he had learned from his magic books the secret and the value of this wonderful lamp, the owner of which would be made richer than any earthly ruler, and hence his journey to China.

His art had also told him that he was not permitted to take it himself, but must receive it as a voluntary gift from the hands of another person. Hence he employed young Aladdin, and hoped by a mixture of kindness and authority to make him obedient to his word and will. When he found that his attempt had failed, he set out to return to Africa, but avoided the town, lest any person who had seen him leave in company with Aladdin should make inquiries after the youth.

Aladdin being suddenly enveloped in darkness, cried, and called out to his uncle to tell him he was ready to give him the lamp; but in vain, since his cries could not be heard. He descended to the bottom of the steps, with a design to get into the palace, but the door, which was opened before by enchantment, was now shut by the same means. He then redoubled his cries and tears, sat down on the steps without any hopes of ever seeing light again, and in an expectation of passing from the present darkness to a speedy death. In this great emergency he said, "There is no strength or power but in the great and high God"; and in joining his hands to pray he rubbed the ring which the magician had put on his finger. Immediately a genie of frightful aspect appeared, and said, "What wouldst thou have? I am ready to obey thee.

I serve him who possesses the ring on thy finger; I and the other slaves of that ring." At another time Aladdin would have been frightened at the sight of so extraordinary a figure, but the danger he was in made him answer without hesitation, "Whoever thou art, deliver me from this place."

He had no sooner spoken these words than he found himself on the very spot where the magician had last left him, and no sign of cave or opening, nor disturbance of the earth. Returning God thanks to find himself once more in the world, he made the best of his way home.

When he got within his mother's door, the joy to see her and his weakness for want of sustenance made him so faint that he remained for a long time as dead. As soon as he recovered he related to his mother all that had happened to him, and they were both very vehement in their complaints of the cruel magician. Aladdin slept very soundly till late the next morning, when the first thing he said to his mother was that he wanted something to eat, and wished she would give him his breakfast.

"Alas! child," said she, "I have not a bit of bread to give you: you ate up all the provisions I had in the house yesterday; but I have a little cotton, which I have spun; I will go and sell it, and buy bread and something for our dinner."

"Mother," replied Aladdin, "keep your cotton for another time, and give me the lamp I brought home with me yesterday; I will go and sell it, and the money I shall get for it will serve both for breakfast and dinner, and perhaps supper too."

Aladdin's mother took the lamp, and said to her son, "Here it is, but it is very dirty; if it was a little cleaner I believe it would bring something more." She took some fine sand and water to clean it; but had no sooner begun to rub it than in an instant a hideous genie of gigantic size appeared before her, and said to her in a voice of thunder, "What wouldst thou have? I am ready to obey thee as thy slave, and the slave of all those who have that lamp in their hands; I and the other slaves of the lamp."

Aladdin's mother, terrified at the sight of the genie, fainted; when Aladdin, who had seen such a phantom in the cavern, snatched the lamp out of his mother's hand, and said to the genie boldly, "I am hungry; bring me something to eat." The genie disappeared immediately, and in an instant returned with a large silver tray, holding twelve covered dishes of the same metal, which contained the most delicious viands; six large white bread cakes on two plates, two flagons of wine, and two silver cups. All these he placed upon a carpet, and disappeared; this was done before Aladdin's mother recovered from her swoon.

Aladdin had fetched some water, and sprinkled it in her face to recover her. Whether that or the smell of the meat effected her cure, it was not long before she came to herself. "Mother" said Aladdin, "be not afraid; get up and eat; here is what will put you in heart, and at the same time satisfy my extreme hunger."

Aladdin Story part - 5

His mother was much surprised to see the great tray, twelve dishes, six loaves, the two flagons and cups, and to smell the savory odor which exhaled from the dishes. "Child," said she, "to whom are we obliged for this great plenty and liberality? Has the sultan been made acquainted with our poverty, and had compassion on us?" "It is no matter, mother," said Aladdin, "let us sit down and eat; for you have almost as much need of a good breakfast as myself; when we have done, I will tell you."

Accordingly, both mother and son sat down, and ate with the better relish as the table was so well furnished. But all the time Aladdin's mother could not forbear looking at and admiring the tray and dishes, though she could not judge whether they were silver or any other metal, and the novelty more than the value attracted her attention.

The mother and son sat at breakfast till it was dinner time, and then they thought it would be best to put the two meals together; yet after this they found they should have enough left for supper, and two meals for the next day.

When Aladdin's mother had taken away and set by what was left, she went and sat down by her son on the sofa, saying, "I expect now that you should satisfy my impatience, and tell me exactly what passed between the genie and you while I was in a swoon"; which he readily complied with.

She was in as great amazement at what her son told her as at the appearance of the genie; and said to him, "But, son, what have we to do with genies? I never heard that any of my acquaintance had ever seen one. How came that vile genie to address himself to me, and not to you, to whom he had appeared before in the cave?" "Mother," answered Aladdin, "the genie you saw is not the one who appeared to me. If you remember, he that I first saw called himself the slave of the ring on my finger; and this you saw called himself the slave of the lamp you had in your hand; but

I believe you did not hear him, for I think you fainted as soon as he began to speak."

"What!" cried the mother, "was your lamp, then, the occasion of that cursed genie's addressing himself rather to me than to you? Ah! my son, take it out of my sight, and put it where you please. I had rather you would sell it than run the hazard of being frightened to death again by touching it; and if you would take my advice you would part also with the ring, and not have anything to do with genies, who, as our prophet has told us, are only devils."

"With your leave, mother," replied Aladdin, "I shall now take care how I sell a lamp which may be so serviceable both to you and me. That false and wicked magician would not have undertaken so long a journey to secure this wonderful lamp if he had not known its value to exceed that of gold and silver. And since we have honestly come by it, let us make a profitable use of it, without making any great show, and exciting the envy and jealousy of our neighbors.

However, since the genies frighten you so much I will take it out of your sight, and put it where I may find it when I want it. The ring I cannot resolve to part with; for without that you had never seen me again; and though I am alive now, perhaps, if it were gone, I might not be so some moments hence; therefore, I hope you will give me leave to keep it, and to wear it always on my finger."

Aladdin's mother replied that he might do what he pleased; for her part she would have nothing to do with genies, and never say anything more about them.

By the next night they had eaten all the provisions the genie had brought; and the next day Aladdin, who could not bear the thought of hunger, putting one of the silver dishes under his vest, went out early to sell it, and addressing himself to a Jew whom he met in the streets, took him aside, and pulling out the plate, asked him if he would buy it. The cunning Jew took the dish, examined it, and as soon as he found that it was good silver asked Aladdin at how much he valued it. Aladdin, who had never been used to such traffic, told him he would trust to his judgment and honor.

The Jew was somewhat confounded at this plain dealing; and doubting whether Aladdin understood the material or the full value of what he offered to sell, took a piece of gold out of his purse and gave it him, though it was but the sixtieth part of the worth of the plate. Aladdin, taking the money very eagerly, retired with so much haste that the Jew, not content with the exorbitancy of his profit, was vexed he had not penetrated into his ignorance, and was going to run after him, to endeavor to get some change out of the piece of gold; but he ran so fast, and had got so far, that it would have been impossible for him to overtake him.

Before Aladdin went home he called at a baker's, bought some cakes of bread, changed his money, and on his return gave the rest to his mother, who went and purchased provisions enough to last them some time. After this manner they lived, till Aladdin had sold the twelve dishes singly, as necessity pressed, to the Jew, for the same money; who, after the first time, durst not offer him less for fear of losing so good a bargain. When he had sold the last dish he had recourse to the tray, which weighed ten times as much as the dishes, and would have carried it to his old purchaser, but that it was too large and cumbersome; therefore he was obliged to bring him home with him to his mother's, where, after the Jew had examined the weight of the tray, he laid down ten pieces of gold, with which Aladdin was very well satisfied.

When all the money was spent, Aladdin had recourse again to the lamp. He took it in his hand, looked for that part where his mother had rubbed it with the sand, rubbed it also, when the genie immediately appeared, and said, "What wouldst thou have? I am ready to obey thee as thy slave, and the slave of all those who have that lamp in their hands; I and the other slaves of the lamp." "I am hungry," said Aladdin; "bring me something to eat." The genie disappeared, and presently returned with a tray, the same number of covered dishes as before, set them down, and vanished.

As soon as Aladdin found that their provisions were again expended, he took one of the dishes, and went to look for his Jew chapman; but passing by a goldsmith's shop, the goldsmith perceiving him called to him and said, "My lad, I imagine that you have something to sell to the Jew, whom I often see you visit; but perhaps you do not know that he is the greatest rogue even among the Jews.

I will give you the full worth of what you have to sell, or I will direct you to other merchants who will not cheat you."

This offer induced Aladdin to pull his plate from under his vest and show it to the goldsmith, who at first sight saw that it was made of the finest silver, and asked him if he had sold such as that to the Jew; when Aladdin told him that he had sold him twelve such, for a piece of gold each. "What a villain!" cried the goldsmith. "But," added he, "my son, what is past cannot be recalled. By showing you the value of this plate, which is of the finest silver we use in our shops, I will let you see how much the Jew has cheated you."

The goldsmith took a pair of scales, weighed the dish, and assured him that his plate would fetch by weight sixty pieces of gold, which he offered to pay down immediately.Aladdin thanked him for his fair dealing, and never after went to any other person.

Though Aladdin and his mother had an inexhaustible treasure in their lamp, and might have had whatever they wished for, yet they lived with the same frugality as before, and it may easily be supposed that the money for which Aladdin had sold the dishes and tray was sufficient to maintain them some time.

During this interval, Aladdin frequented the shops of the principal merchants, where they sold cloth of gold and silver, linens, silk stuffs, and jewelry, and oftentimes joining in their conversation, acquired a knowledge of the world and a desire to improve himself. By his acquaintance among the jewellers he came to know that the fruits which he had gathered when he took the lamp were, instead of colored glass, stones of inestimable value; but he had the prudence not to mention this to anyone, not even to his mother.

One day as Aladdin was walking about the town he heard an order proclaimed commanding the people to shut up their shops and houses, and keep within doors while the Princess Buddir al Buddoor, the sultan's daughter, went to the bath and returned.

This proclamation inspired Aladdin with an eager desire to see the princess's face, which he determined to gratify by placing himself behind the door of the bath, so that he could not fail to see her face.

Aladdin had not long concealed himself before the princess came. She was attended by a great crowd of ladies, slaves, and mutes, who walked on each side and behind her. When she came within three or four paces of the door of the bath, she took off her veil, and gave Aladdin an opportunity of a full view of her face.

The princess was a noted beauty: her eyes were large, lively, and sparkling; her smile bewitching; her nose faultless; her mouth small; her lips vermilion. It is not therefore surprising that Aladdin, who had never before seen such a blaze of charms, was dazzled and enchanted.

After the princess had passed by, and entered the bath, Aladdin quitted his hiding-place and went home. His mother perceived him to be more thoughtful and melancholy than usual, and asked what had happened to make him so, or if he was ill. He then told his mother all his adventure, and concluded by declaring, "I love the princess more than I can express, and am resolved that I will ask her in marriage of the sultan."

Aladdin's mother listened with surprise to what her son told her; but when he talked of asking the princess in marriage, she laughed aloud. "Alas! child," said she, "what are you thinking of? You must be mad to talk thus."

"I assure you, mother," replied Aladdin, "that I am not mad, but in my right senses. I foresaw that you would reproach me with folly and extravagance; but I must tell you once more that I am resolved to demand the princess of the sultan in marriage, nor do I despair of success. I have the slaves of the Lamp and of the Ring to help me, and you know how powerful their aid is.

And I have another secret to tell you: those pieces of glass, which I got
from the trees in the garden of the subterranean palace, are jewels of
inestimable value, and fit for the greatest monarchs. All the precious
stones the jewellers have in Bagdad are not to be compared to mine for
size or beauty; and I am sure that the offer of them will secure the favor of
the sultan. You have a large porcelain dish fit to hold them; fetch it, and let
us see how they will look, when we have arranged them according to their
different colors."

Aladdin Story part - 6

- Aladdin Story part - 6

Aladdin's mother brought the china dish, when he took the jewels out of the two purses in which he had kept them, and placed them in order according to his fancy. But the brightness and lustre they emitted in the daytime, and the variety of the colors, so dazzled the eyes both of mother and son that they were astonished beyond measure. Aladdin's mother, emboldened by the sight of these rich jewels, and fearful lest her son should be guilty of greater extravagance, complied with his request, and promised to go early in the next morning to the palace of the sultan. Aladdin rose before daybreak, awakened his mother, pressing her to go to the sultan's palace, and to get admittance, if possible, before the grand vizier, the other viziers, and the great officers of state went in to take their seats in the divan, where the sultan always attended in person.

Aladdin's mother took the china dish, in which they had put the jewels the day before, wrapped it in two fine napkins, and set forward for the sultan's palace. When she came to the gates, the grand vizier, the other viziers, and most distinguished lords of the court were just gone in; but notwithstanding the crowd of people was great, she got into the divan, a spacious hall, the entrance into which was very magnificent. She placed herself just before the sultan, grand vizier, and the great lords, who sat in council on his right and left hand. Several causes were called, according to their order, pleaded and adjudged, until the time the divan generally broke up, when the sultan, rising, returned to his apartment, attended by the grand vizier; the other viziers and ministers of state then retired, as also did all those whose business had called them thither.

Aladdin's mother, seeing the sultan retire, and all the people depart, judged rightly that he would not sit again that day, and resolved to go home; and on her arrival said, with much simplicity, "Son, I have seen the sultan, and am very well persuaded he has seen me too, for I placed myself just before him; but he was so much taken up with those who attended on all sides of him, that I pitied him and wondered at his patience. At last I believe he was heartily tired, for he rose up suddenly, and would not hear a great many who were ready prepared to speak to him, but went away, at which I was well pleased, for indeed I began to lose all patience, and was extremely fatigued with staying so long. But there is no harm done: I will go again tomorrow; perhaps the sultan may not be so busy."

The next morning she repaired to the sultan's palace with the present, as early as the day before; but when she came there she found the gates of the divan shut. She went six times afterward on the days appointed, placed herself always directly before the sultan, but with as little success as the first morning.

On the sixth day, however, after the divan was broken up, when the sultan returned to his own apartment, he said to his grand vizier, "I have for some time observed a certain woman, who attends constantly every day that I give audience, with something wrapped up in a napkin; she always stands up from the beginning to the breaking up of the audience, and affects to place herself just before me. If this woman comes to our next audience, do not fail to call her, that I may hear what she has to say." The grand vizier made answer by lowering his hand, and then lifting it up above his head, signifying his willingness to lose it if he failed.

On the next audience day, when Aladdin's mother went to the divan, and placed herself in front of the sultan as usual, the grand vizier immediately called the chief of the mace-bearers, and, pointing to her, bade him bring her before the sultan.

The old woman at once followed the mace-bearer, and when she reached the sultan, bowed her head down to the carpet which covered the platform of the throne, and remained in that posture till he bade her rise, which she had no sooner done than he said to her, "Good woman, I have observed you to stand many days, from the beginning to the rising of the divan; what business brings you here?"

After these words, Aladdin's mother prostrated herself a second time, and, when she arose, said, "Monarch of monarchs I beg of you to pardon the boldness of my petition, and to assure me of your pardon and forgiveness."

"Well,". replied the sultan, "I will forgive you, be it what it may, and no hurt shall come to you. Speak boldly."

When Aladdin's mother had taken all these precautions for fear of the sultan's anger, she told him faithfully the errand on which her son had sent her, and the event which led to his making so bold a request in spite of all her remonstrances.

The sultan hearkened to this discourse without showing the least anger; but, before he gave her any answer, asked her what she had brought tied up in the napkin. She took the china dish, which she had set down at the foot of the throne, untied it, and presented it to the sultan.

The sultan's amazement and surprise were inexpressible when he saw so many large, beautiful, and valuable jewels collected in the dish. He remained for some time lost in admiration. At last, when he had recovered himself, he received the present from Aladdin's mother's hand, saying, "How rich! how beautiful!" After he had admired and handled all the jewels one after another, he turned to his grand vizier, and, showing him the dish, said, "Behold! admire! wonder! and confess that your eyes never beheld jewels so rich and beautiful before!" The vizier was charmed. "Well," continued the sultan, "what sayest thou to such a present? Is it not worthy of the princess my daughter? And ought I not to bestow her on one who values her at so great a price?" "I cannot but own," replied the grand vizier, "that the present is worthy of the princess; but I beg of your majesty to grant me three months before you come to a final resolution. I hope before that time my son, whom you have regarded with your favor, will be able to make a nobler present than this Aladdin, who is an entire stranger to your majesty."

The sultan granted his request, and he said to the old woman, "Good woman, go home, and tell your son that I agree to the proposal you have made me; but I cannot marry the princess my daughter for three months. At the expiration of that time come again."

Aladdin's mother returned home much more gratified than she had expected, and told her son with much joy the condescending answer she had received from the sultan's own mouth; and that she was to come to the divan again that day three months.

Aladdin thought himself the most happy of all men at hearing this news, and thanked his mother for the pains she had taken in the affair, the good success of which was of so great importance to his peace that he counted every day, week, and even hour as it passed. When two of the three months were passed, his mother one evening, having no oil in the house, went out to buy some, and found a general rejoicingâ€"the houses dressed with foliage, silks, and carpeting, and every one striving to show their joy according to their ability.

The streets were crowded with officers in habits of ceremony, mounted on horses richly caparisoned, each attended by a great many footmen. Aladdin's mother asked the oil merchant what was the meaning of all this preparation of public festivity. "Whence came you, good woman," said he, "that you don't know that the grand vizier's son is to marry the princess Buddir al Buddoor, the sultan's daughter, to-night? She will presently return from the bath; and these officers whom you see are to assist at the cavalcade to the palace, where the ceremony is to be solemnized."

Aladdin's mother on hearing this news ran home very quickly. "Child," cried she, "you are undone; the sultan's fine promise will come to naught! This night the grand vizier's son is to marry the Princess Buddir al Buddoor."

At this account Aladdin was thunderstruck, and he bethought himself of the lamp, and of the genie who had promised to obey him; and without indulging in idle words against the sultan, the vizier, or his son, he determined, if possible, to prevent the marriage.

When Aladdin had got into his chamber, he took the lamp, rubbed it in the same place as before, when immediately the genie appeared, and said to him, "What wouldst thou have? I am ready to obey thee as thy slave; I and the other slaves of the lamp." "Hear me," said Aladdin. "Thou hast hitherto obeyed me; but now I am about to impose on thee a harder task. The sultan's daughter, who was promised me as my bride, is this night married to the son of the grand vizier. Bring them both hither to me immediately they retire to their bedchamber."

"Master," replied the genie, "I obey you."

Aladdin supped with his mother as was their wont, and then went to his own apartment, and sat up to await the return of the genie, according to his commands.

In the meantime, the festivities in honor of the princess's marriage were conducted in the sultan's palace with great magnificence. The ceremonies were at last brought to a conclusion, and the princess and the son of the vizier retired to the bedchamber prepared for them. No sooner had they entered it and dismissed their attendants, than the genie, the faithful slave of the lamp, to the great amazement and alarm of the bride and bridegroom, took up the bed, and, by an agency invisible to them, transported it in an instant into Aladdin's chamber, where he set it down. "Remove the bridegroom," said Aladdin to the genie, "and keep him a prisoner till to-morrow dawn, and then return with him here." On Aladdin being left alone with the princess, he endeavored to assuage her fears, and explained to her the treachery practised upon him by the sultan her father.

He then laid himself down beside her, putting a drawn scimitar between them, to show that he was determined to secure her safety, and to treat her with the utmost possible respect. At break of day the genie appeared at the appointed hour, bringing back the bridegroom, whom, by breathing upon, he had left motionless and entranced at the door of Aladdin's chamber during the night; and, at Aladdin's command, transported the couch with the bride and bridegroom on it, by the same invisible agency, into the palace of the sultan.

At the instant that the genie had set down the couch with the bride and bridegroom in their own chamber, the sultan came to the door to offer his good wishes to his daughter.

Aladdin Story part - 7

• Aladdin Story part - 7

The grand vizier's son, who was almost perished with cold by standing in his thin under-garment all night, no sooner heard the knocking at the door than he got out of bed and ran into the robing chamber, where he had undressed himself the night before.

The sultan, having opened the door, went to the bedside, kissed the princess on the forehead, but was extremely surprised to see her look so melancholy. She only cast at him a sorrowful look, expressive of great affliction. He suspected there was something extraordinary in this silence, and thereupon went immediately to the sultaness's apartment, told her in what a state he found the princess, and how she had received him. "Sire," said the sultaness, "I will go and see her; she will not receive me in the same manner."

The princess received her mother with sighs and tears, and signs of deep dejection. At last, upon her pressing on her the duty of telling her all her thoughts, she gave to the sultaness a precise description of all that happened to her during the night; on which the sultaness enjoined on her the necessity of silence and discretion, as no one would give credence to so strange a tale. The grand vizier's son, elated with the honor of being the sultan's son-in-law, kept silence on his part, and the events of the night were not allowed to cast the least gloom on the festivities on the following day, in continued celebration of the royal marriage.

When night came the bride and bridegroom were again attended to their chamber with the same ceremonies as on the preceding evening. Aladdin, knowing that this would be so, had already given his commands to the genie of the lamp; and no sooner were they alone than their bed was removed in the same mysterious manner as on the preceding evening; and having passed the night in the same unpleasant way, they were in the morning conveyed to the palace of the sultan. Scarcely had they been replaced in their apartment than the sultan came to make his compliments to his daughter, when the princess could no longer conceal from him the unhappy treatment she had been subjected to, and told him all that had happened, as she had already related it to her mother.

The sultan, on hearing these strange tidings, consulted with the grand vizier; and finding from him that his son had been subjected to even worse treatment by an invisible agency, he determined to declare the marriage to be cancelled, and all the festivities, which were yet to last for several days, to be countermanded and terminated.

This sudden change in the mind of the sultan gave rise to various speculations and reports. Nobody but Aladdin knew the secret, and he kept it with the most scrupulous silence; and neither the sultan nor the grand vizier, who had forgotten Aladdin and his request, had the least thought that he had any hand in the strange adventures that befel the bride and bridegroom.

On the very day that the three months contained in the sultan's promise expired, the mother of Aladdin again went to the palace, and stood in the same place in the divan. The sultan knew her again, and directed his vizier to have her brought before him.

After having prostrated herself she made answer, in reply to the sultan: "Sire, I come at the end of three months to ask of you the fulfilment of the promise you made to my son." The sultan little thought the request of Aladdin's mother was made to him in earnest, or that he would hear any more of the matter. He therefore took counsel with his vizier, who suggested that the sultan should attach such conditions to the marriage that no one in the humble condition of Aladdin could possibly fulfil.

In accordance with this suggestion of the vizier, the sultan replied to the mother of Aladdin: "Good woman, it is true sultans ought to abide by their word, and I am ready to keep mine, by making your son happy in marriage with the princess my daughter. But as I cannot marry her without some further proof of your son being able to support her in royal state, you may tell him I will fulfil my promise as soon as he shall send me forty trays of massy gold, full of the same sort of jewels you have already made me a present of, and carried by the like number of black slaves, who shall be led by as many young and handsome white slaves, all dressed magnificently. On these conditions I am ready to bestow the princess my daughter upon him; therefore, good woman, go and tell him so, and I will wait till you bring me his answer."

Aladdin's mother prostrated herself a second time before the sultan's throne, and retired. On her way home she laughed within herself at her son's foolish imagination. "Where," said she, "can he get so many large gold trays, and such precious stones to fill them? It is altogether out of his power, and I believe he will not be much pleased with my embassy this time." When she came home, full of these thoughts, she told Aladdin all the circumstances of her interview with the sultan, and the conditions on which he consented to the marriage. "The sultan expects your answer immediately," said she; and then added, laughing, "I believe he may wait long enough!"

"Not so long, mother, as you imagine," replied Aladdin. "This demand is a mere trifle, and will prove no bar to my marriage with the princess. I will prepare at once to satisfy his request."

Aladdin retired to his own apartment and summoned the genie of the lamp, and required him to immediately prepare and present the gift, before the sultan closed his morning audience, according to the terms in which it had been prescribed. The genie professed his obedience to the owner of the lamp, and disappeared. Within a very short time, a train of forty black slaves, led by the same number of white slaves, appeared opposite the house in which Aladdin lived. Each black slave carried on his head a basin of massy gold, full of pearls, diamonds, rubies, and emeralds. Aladdin then addressed his mother; "Madam, pray lose no time; before the sultan and the divan rise, I would have you return to the palace with this present as the dowry demanded for the princess, that he may judge by my diligence and exactness of the ardent and sincere desire I have to procure myself the honor of this alliance."

As soon as this magnificent procession, with Aladdin's mother at its head, had begun to march from Aladdin's house, the whole city was filled with the crowds of people desirous to see so grand a sight. The graceful bearing, elegant form, and wonderful likeness of each slave; their grave walk at an equal distance from each other; the lustre of their jewelled girdles, and the brilliancy of the aigrettes of precious stones in their turbans, excited the greatest admiration in the spectators.

As they had to pass through several streets to the palace, the whole length of the way was lined with files of spectators. Nothing, indeed, was ever seen so beautiful and brilliant in the sultan's palace, and the richest robes of the emirs of his court were not to be compared to the costly dresses of these slaves, whom they supposed to be kings.

As the sultan, who had been informed of their approach, had given orders for them to be admitted, they met with no obstacle, but went into the divan in regular order, one part turning to the right, and the other to the left. After they were all entered, and had formed a semi-circle before the sultan's throne, the black slaves laid the golden trays on the carpet, prostrated themselves, touching the carpet with their foreheads, and at the same time the white slaves did the same. When they rose, the black slaves uncovered the trays, and then all stood with their arms crossed over their breasts.

In the meantime, Aladdin's mother advanced to the foot of the throne, and having prostrated herself, said to the sultan, "Sire, my son knows this present is much below the notice of Princess Buddir al Buddoor; but hopes, nevertheless, that your majesty will accept of it, and make it agreeable to the princess, and with the greater confidence since he has endeavored to conform to the conditions you were pleased to impose."

The sultan, overpowered at the sight of such more than royal magnificence, replied without hesitation to the words of Aladdin's mother: "Go and tell your son that I wait with open arms to embrace him; and the more haste he makes to come and receive the princess my daughter from my hands, the greater pleasure he will do me." As soon as Aladdin's mother had retired, the sultan put an end to the audience; and rising from his throne, ordered that the princess's attendants should come and carry the trays into their mistress's apartment, whither he went himself to examine them with her at his leisure. The fourscore slaves were conducted into the palace; and the sultan, telling the princess of their magnificent apparel, ordered them to be brought before her apartment, that she might see through the lattices he had not exaggerated in his account of them.

In the meantime Aladdin's mother reached home, and showed in her air and countenance the good news she brought her son. "My son," said she, "you may rejoice you are arrived at the height of your desires. The sultan has declared that you shall marry the Princess Buddir al Buddoor. He waits for you with impatience."

Aladdin, enraptured with this news, made his mother very little reply, but retired to his chamber. There he rubbed his lamp, and the obedient genie appeared. "Genie," said Aladdin, "convey me at once to a bath, and supply me with the richest and most magnificent robe ever worn by a monarch."

No sooner were the words out of his mouth than the genie rendered him, as well as himself, invisible, and transported him into a hummum of the finest marble of all sorts of colors, where he was undressed, without seeing by whom, in a magnificent and spacious hall. He was then well rubbed and washed with various scented waters. After he had passed through several degrees of heat, he came out quite a different man from what he was before. His skin was clear as that of a child, his body lightsome and free; and when he returned into the hall, he found, instead of his own poor raiment, a robe the magnificence of which astonished him.

The genie helped him to dress, and when he had done, transported him back to his own chamber, where he asked him if he had any other commands. "Yes," answered Aladdin; "bring me a charger that surpasses in beauty and goodness the best in the sultan's stables, with a saddle, bridle, and other caparisons to correspond with his value. Furnish also twenty slaves, as richly clothed as those who carried the present to the sultan, to walk by my side and follow me, and twenty more to go before me in two ranks. Besides these, bring my mother six women slaves to attend her, as richly dressed at least as any of the Princess Buddir al Buddoor's, each carrying a complete dress fit for any sultaness. I want also ten thousand pieces of gold in ten purses; go, and make haste,"

As soon as Aladdin had given these orders, the genie disappeared, but presently returned with the horse, the forty slaves, ten of whom carried each a purse containing ten thousand pieces of gold, and six women slaves, each carrying on her head a different dress for Aladdin's mother, wrapped up in a piece of silver tissue, and presented them all to Aladdin.

He presented the six women slaves to his mother, telling her they were her slaves, and that the dresses they had brought were for her use. Of the ten purses Aladdin took four, which he gave to his mother, telling her those were to supply her with necessaries; the other six he left in the hands of the slaves who brought them, with an order to throw them by handfuls among the people as they went to the sultan's palace. The six slaves who carried the purses he ordered likewise to march before him, three on the right hand and three on the left.

When Aladdin had thus prepared himself for his first interview with the sultan, he dismissed the genie, and immediately mounting his charger, began his march, and though he never was on horseback before, appeared with a grace the most experienced horseman might envy. The innumerable concourse of people through whom he passed made the air echo with their acclamations, especially every time the six slaves who carried the purses threw handfuls of gold among the populace.

Aladdin Story part - 8

- Aladdin Story part - 8

On Aladdin's arrival at the palace, the sultan was surprised to find him more richly and magnificently robed than he had ever been himself, and was impressed with his good looks and dignity of manner, which were so different from what he expected in the son of one so humble as Aladdin's mother. He embraced him with all the demonstrations of joy, and when he would have fallen at his feet, held him by the hand, and made him sit near his throne. He shortly after led him, amid the sounds of trumpets, hautboys, and all kinds of music, to a magnificent entertainment, at which the sultan and Aladdin ate by themselves, and the great lords of the court, according to their rank and dignity, sat at different tables. After the feast the sultan sent for the chief cadi, and commanded him to draw up a contract of marriage between the Princess Buddir al Buddoor and Aladdin. When the contract had been drawn, the sultan asked Aladdin if he would stay in the palace and complete the ceremonies of the marriage that day.

"Sire," said Aladdin, "though great is my impatience to enter on the honor granted me by your majesty, yet I beg you to permit me first to build a palace worthy to receive the princess your daughter. I pray you to grant me sufficient ground near your palace, and I will have it completed with the utmost expedition."

The sultan granted Aladdin his request, and again embraced him. After which he took his leave with as much politeness as if he had been bred up and had always lived at court.

Aladdin returned home in the order he had come, amid the acclamations of the people, who wished him all happiness and prosperity. As soon as he dismounted, he retired to his own chamber, took the lamp, and summoned the genie as usual, who professed his allegiance.

"Genie," said Aladdin, "build me a palace fit to receive the Princess Buddir al Buddoor. Let its materials be made of nothing less than porphyry, jasper, agate, lapis-lazuli, and the finest marble. Let its walls be massive gold and silver bricks laid alternately. Let each front contain six windows, and let the lattices of these (except one, which must be left unfinished) be enriched with diamonds, rubies, and emeralds, so that they shall exceed everything of the kind ever seen in the world. Let there be an inner and outer court in front of the palace, and a spacious garden; but, above all things, provide a safe treasure-house, and fill it with gold and silver. Let there be also kitchens and storehouses, stables full of the finest horses, with their equerries and grooms, and hunting equipage, officers, attendants, and slaves, both men and women, to form a retinue for the princess and myself. Go and execute my wishes."

When Aladdin gave these commands to the genie the sun was set. The next morning at daybreak the genie presented himself, and having obtained Aladdin's consent, transported him in a moment to the palace he had made. The genie led him through all the apartments, where he found officers and slaves, habited according to their rank and the services to which they were appointed. The genie then showed him the treasury, which was opened by a treasurer, where Aladdin saw large vases of different sizes, piled up to the top with money, ranged all round the chamber. The genie thence led him to the stables, where were some of the finest horses in the world, and the grooms busy in dressing them; from thence they went to the storehouses, which were filled with all things necessary, both for food and ornament.

When Aladdin had examined every portion of the palace, and particularly the hall with the four-and-twenty windows, and found it to far exceed his fondest expectations, he said, "Genie, there is one thing wantingâ€"a fine carpet for the princess to walk upon from the sultan's palace to mine. Lay one down immediately."

The genie disappeared, and Aladdin saw what he desired executed in an instant. The genie then returned and carried him to his own home.

When the sultan's porters came to open the gates they were amazed to find what had been an unoccupied garden filled up with a magnificent palace, and a splendid carpet extending to it all the way from the sultan's palace. They told the strange tidings to the grand vizier, who informed the sultan, who exclaimed, "It must be Aladdin's palace, which I gave him leave to build for my daughter. He has wished to surprise us, and let us see what wonders can be done in only one night."

Aladdin, on his being conveyed by the genie to his own home, requested his mother to go to the Princess Buddir al Buddoor, and tell her that the palace would be ready for her reception in the evening. She went, attended by her women slaves, in the same order as on the preceding day. Shortly after her arrival at the princess's apartment, the sultan himself came in, and was surprised to find her, whom he knew as his suppliant at his divan in such humble guise, to be now more richly and sumptuously attired than his own daughter. This gave him a higher opinion of Aladdin, who took such care of his mother, and made her share his wealth and honors.

Shortly after her departure Aladdin, mounting his horse, and attended by his retinue of magnificent attendants, left his paternal home forever, and went to the palace in the same pomp as on the day before. Nor did he forget to take with him the wonderful lamp, to which he owed all his good-fortune, nor to wear the ring which was given him as a talisman. The sultan entertained Aladdin with the utmost magnificence, and at night, on the conclusion of the marriage ceremonies, the princess took leave of the sultan her father.

Bands of music led the procession, followed by a hundred state ushers, and the like number of black mutes, in two files, with their officers at their head. Four hundred of the sultan's young pages carried flambeaux on each side, which, together with the illuminations of the sultan's and Aladdin's palaces, made it as light as day. In this order the princess, conveyed in her litter, and accompanied also by Aladdin's mother, carried in a superb litter and attended by her women slaves, proceeded on the carpet which was spread from the sultan's palace to that of Aladdin.

On her arrival Aladdin was ready to receive her at the entrance, and led her into a large hall, illuminated with an infinite number of wax candles, where a noble feast was served up. The dishes were of massy gold, and contained the most delicate viands. The vases, basins, and goblets were gold also, and of exquisite workmanship, and all the other ornaments and embellishments of the hall were answerable to this display. The princess, dazzled to see so much riches collected in one place, said to Aladdin: "I thought, prince, that nothing in the world was so beautiful as the sultan my father's palace, but the sight of this hall alone is sufficient to show I was deceived."

When the supper was ended, there entered a company of female dancers, who performed, according to the custom of the country, singing at the same time verses in praise of the bride and bridegroom.About midnight Aladdin's mother conducted the bride to the nuptial apartment, and he soon after retired.

The next morning the attendants of Aladdin presented themselves to dress him, and brought him another habit, as rich and magnificent as that worn the day before. He then ordered one of the horses to be got ready, mounted him, and went in the midst of a large troop of slaves to the sultan's palace, to entreat him to take a repast in the princess's palace, attended by his grand vizier and all the lords of his court. The sultan consented with pleasure, rose up immediately, and, preceded by the principal officers of his palace, and followed by all the great lords of his court, accompanied Aladdin.

The nearer the sultan approached Aladdin's palace the more he was struck with its beauty; but when he entered it, came into the hall, and saw the windows enriched with diamonds, rubies, emeralds, all large, perfect stones, he was completely surprised, and said to his son-in-law: "This palace is one of the wonders of the world; for where in all the world besides shall we find walls built of massy gold and silver, and diamonds, rubies, and emeralds composing the windows? But what most surprises me is that a hall of this magnificence should be left with one of its windows incomplete and unfinished." "Sire," answered Aladdin, "the omission was by design, since I wished that you should have the glory of finishing this hall." "I take your intention kindly," said the sultan, "and will give orders about it immediately."

After the sultan had finished this magnificent entertainment provided for him and for his court by Aladdin, he was informed that the jewellers and goldsmiths attended; upon which he returned to the hall, and showed them the window which was unfinished. "I sent for you," said he, "to fit up this window in as great perfection as the rest. Examine them well, and make all the despatch you can."

The jewellers and goldsmiths examined the three-and-twenty windows with great attention, and after they had consulted together, to know what each could furnish, they returned, and presented themselves before the sultan, whose principal jeweller, undertaking to speak for the rest, said: "Sire, we are all willing to exert our utmost care and industry to obey you; but among us all we cannot furnish jewels enough for so great a work." "I have more than are necessary," said the sultan; "come to my palace, and you shall choose what may answer your purpose."

When the sultan returned to his palace, he ordered his jewels to be brought out, and the jewellers took a great quantity, particularly those Aladdin had made him a present of, which they soon used, without making any great advance in their work. They came again several times for more, and in a month's time had not finished half their work. In short, they used all the jewels the sultan had, and borrowed of the vizier, but yet the work was not half done.

Aladdin, who knew that all the sultan's endeavors to make this window like the rest were in vain, sent for the jewellers and goldsmiths, and not only commanded them to desist from their work, but ordered them to undo what they had begun, and to carry all their jewels back to the sultan and to the vizier. They undid in a few hours what they had been six weeks about, and retired, leaving Aladdin alone in the hall. He took the lamp, which he carried about him, rubbed it, and presently the genie appeared. "Genie," said Aladdin, "I ordered thee to leave one of the four- and-twenty windows of this hall imperfect, and thou hast executed my commands punctually; now I would have thee make it like the rest." The genie immediately disappeared. Aladdin went out of the hall, and returning soon after, found the window, as he wished it to be, like the others.

In the meantime, the jewellers and goldsmiths repaired to the palace, and were introduced into the sultan's presence, where the chief jeweller presented the precious stones which he had brought back. The sultan asked them if Aladdin had given them any reason for so doing, and they answering that he had given them none, he ordered a horse to be brought, which he mounted, and rode to his son-in-law's palace, with some few attendants on foot, to inquire why he had ordered the completion of the window to be stopped. Aladdin met him at the gate, and without giving any reply to his inquiries conducted him to the grand saloon, where the sultan, to his great surprise, found the window which was left imperfect to correspond exactly with the others.

He fancied at first that he was mistaken, and examined the two windows on each side, and afterward all the four and twenty; but when he was convinced that the window which several workmen had been so long about was finished in so short a time, he embraced Aladdin and kissed him between his eyes. "My son," said he, "what a man you are to do such surprising things always in the twinkling of an eye! There is not your fellow in the world; the more I know, the more I admire you."

The sultan returned to the palace, and after this went frequently to the window to contemplate and admire the wonderful palace of his son-in-law.

Aladdin did not confine himself in his palace, but went with much state, sometimes to one mosque, and sometimes to another, to prayers, or to visit the grand vizier, or the principal lords of the court. Every time he went out, he caused two slaves, who walked by the side of his horse, to throw handfuls of money among the people as he passed through the streets and squares. This generosity gained him the love and blessings of the people, and it was common for them to swear by his head. Thus Aladdin, while he paid all respect to the sultan, won by his affable behavior and liberality the affections of the people.

Aladdin had conducted himself in this manner several years, when the African magician, who had for some years dismissed him from his recollection, determined to inform himself with certainty whether he perished, as he supposed, in the subterranean cave or not. After he had resorted to a long course of magic ceremonies, and had formed a horoscope by which to ascertain Aladdin's fate, what was his surprise to find the appearances to declare that Aladdin, instead of dying in the cave, had made his escape, and was living in royal splendor, by the aid of the genie of the wonderful lamp!

On the very next day, the magician set out and travelled with the utmost haste to the capital of China, where, on his arrival, he took up his lodging in a khan.

He then quickly learned about the wealth, charities, happiness, and splendid palace of Prince Aladdin. Directly he saw the wonderful fabric, he knew that none but the genies, the slaves of the lamp, could have performed such wonders; and piqued to the quick at Aladdin's high estate, he returned to the khan.

On his return he had recourse to an operation of geomancy to find out where the lamp wasâ€"whether Aladdin carried it about with him, or where he left it. The result of his consultation informed him, to his great joy, that the lamp was in the palace. "Well," said he, rubbing his hands in glee, "I shall have the lamp, and I shall make Aladdin return to his original mean condition."

Aladdin Story part - 9

- Aladdin Story part - 9

The next day the magician learned, from the chief superintendent of the khan where he lodged, that Aladdin had gone on a hunting expedition, which was to last for eight days, of which only three had expired. The magician wanted to know no more. He resolved at once on his plans. He went to a coppersmith, and asked for a dozen copper lamps: the master of the shop told him he had not so many by him, but if he would have patience till the next day, he would have them ready. The magician appointed his time, and desired him to take care that they should be handsome and well polished.

The next day the magician called for the twelve lamps, paid the man his full price, put them into a basket hanging on his arm, and went directly to Aladdin's palace. As he approached, he began crying, "Who will change old lamps for new ones?" As he went along, a crowd of children collected, who hooted, and thought him, as did all who chanced to be passing by, a madman or a fool, to offer to change new lamps for old ones.

The African magician regarded not their scoffs, hootings, or all they could say to him, but still continued crying, "Who will change old lamps for new ones?" He repeated this so often, walking backward and forward in front of the palace, that the princess, who was then in the hall with the four-and-twenty windows, hearing a man cry something, and seeing a great mob crowding about him, sent one of her women slaves to know what he cried.

The slave returned laughing so heartily that the princess rebuked her. "Madam," answered the slave, laughing still, "who can forbear laughing, to see an old man with a basket on his arm, full of fine new lamps, asking to change them for old ones? The children and mob crowding about him so that he can hardly stir, make all the noise they can in derision of him."

Another female slave, hearing this, said: "Now you speak of lamps, I know not whether the princess may have observed it, but there is an old one upon a shelf of the Prince Aladdin's robing-room, and whoever owns it will not be sorry to find a new one in its stead. If the princess chooses, she may have the pleasure of trying if this old man is so silly as to give a new lamp for an old one, without taking anything for the exchange."

The princess, who knew not the value of this lamp, and the interest that Aladdin had to keep it safe, entered into the pleasantry, and commanded a slave to take it and make the exchange. The slave obeyed, went out of the hall, and no sooner got to the palace gates than he saw the African magician, called to him, and, showing him the old lamp, said, "Give me a new lamp for this."

The magician never doubted but this was the lamp he wanted. There could be no other such in this palace, where every utensil was gold or silver. He snatched it eagerly out of the slave's hand, and, thrusting it as far as he could into his breast, offered him his basket, and bade him choose which he liked best. The slave picked out one, and carried it to the princess; but the change was no sooner made than the place rung with the shouts of the children, deriding the magician's folly.

The African magician stayed no longer near the palace, nor cried any more, "New lamps for old ones!" but made the best of his way to his khan. His end was answered; and by his silence he got rid of the children and the mob.

As soon as he was out of sight of the two palaces, he hastened down the least frequented streets; and, having no more occasion for his lamps or basket, set all down in a spot where nobody saw him. Then going down another street or two, he walked till he came to one of the city gates, and pursuing his way through the suburbs, which were very extensive, at length reached a lonely spot, where he stopped till the darkness of the night, as the most suitable time for the design he had in contemplation. When it became quite dark, he pulled the lamp out of his breast and rubbed it.

At that summons the genie appeared, and said, "What wouldst thou have? I am ready to obey thee as thy slave, and the slave of all those who have that lamp in their hands; both I and the other slaves of the lamp." "I command thee," replied the magician, "to transport me immediately, and the palace which thou and the other slaves of the lamp have built in this dity, with all the people in it, to Africa." The genie made no reply, but, with the assistance of the other genies, the slaves of the lamp, immediately transported him and the palace entire to the spot whither he had been desired to convey it.

Early the next morning when the sultan, according to custom, went to contemplate and admire Aladdin's palace, his amazement was unbounded to find that it could nowhere be seen. He could not comprehend how so large a palace, which he had seen plainly every day for some years, should vanish so soon and not leave the least remains behind. In his perplexity he ordered the grand vizier to be sent for with expedition.

The grand vizier, who in secret bore no goodwill to Aladdin, intimated his suspicion that the palace was built by magic, and that Aladdin had made his hunting excursion an excuse for the removal of his palace with the same suddenness with which it had been erected. He induced the sultan to send a detachment of his guards and to have Aladdin seized as a prisoner of state. On his son-in-law being brought before him, he would not hear a word from him, but ordered him to be put to death.

The decree caused so much discontent among the people, whose affection Aladdin had secured by his largesses and charities, that the sultan, fearful of an insurrection, was obliged to grant him his life. When Aladdin found himself at liberty, he again addressed the sultan: "Sire, I pray you to let me know the crime by which I have thus lost the favor of thy countenance." "Your crime," answered the sultan, "wretched man! do you not know it? Follow me, and I will show you.

" The sultan then took Aladdin into the apartment from whence he was wont to look at and admire his palace, and said, "You ought to know where your palace stood. Look! mind, and tell me what has become of it." Aladdin did so, and, being utterly amazed at the loss of his palace, was speechless. At last, recovering himself, he said: "It is true, I do not see the palace. It is vanished; but I had no concern in its removal.

I beg you to give me forty days, and if in that time I cannot restore it, I will offer my head to be disposed of at your pleasure." "I give you the time you ask, but at the end of the forty days forget not to present yourself before me."

Aladdin went out of the sultan's palace in a condition of exceeding humiliation. The lords who had courted him in the days of his splendor now declined to have any communication with him. For three days he wandered about the city, exciting the wonder and compassion of the multitude, by asking everybody he met if they had seen his palace, or could tell him anything of it. On the third day he wandered into the country, and, as he was approaching a river, he fell down the bank with so much violence that he rubbed the ring which the magician had given him, so hard, by holding on the rock to save himself, that immediately the same genie appeared whom he had seen in the cave where the magician had left him. "What wouldst thou have?" said the genie. "I am ready to obey thee as thy slave, and the slave of all those that have that ring on their finger; both I and the other slaves of the ring."

Aladdin, agreeably surprised at an offer of help so little expected, replied, "Genie, show me where the palace I caused to be built now stands, or transport it back where it first stood." "Your command," answered the genie, "is not wholly in my power; I am only the slave of the ring, and not of the lamp." "I command thee, then," replied Aladdin, "by the power of the ring, to transport me to the spot where my palace stands, in what part of the world soever it may be." These words were no sooner out of his mouth, than the genie transported him into Africa, to the midst of a large plain, where his palace stood, at no great distance from a city, and, placing him exactly under the window of the princess's apartment, left him.

Now it so happened that shortly after Aladdin had been transported by the slave of the ring to the neighborhood of his palace, one of the Attendants of the Princess Buddir al Buddoor, looking through the window, perceived him, and instantly told her mistress. The princess, who could not believe the joyful tidings, hastened herself to the window, and, seeing Aladdin, immediately opened it. The noise of opening the window made Aladdin turn his head that way, and perceiving the princess, he saluted her with an air that expressed his joy.

"To lose no time," said she to him, "I have sent to have the private door opened for you. Enter, and come up."

The private door, which was just under the princess's apartment, was soon opened, and Aladdin conducted up into the chamber. It is impossible to express the joy of both at seeing each other after so cruel a separation. After embracing, and shedding tears of joy, they sat down, and Aladdin said, "I beg of you, princess, to tell me what is become of an old lamp which stood upon a shelf in my robing chamber?"

"Alas!" answered the princess, "I was afraid our misfortune might be owing to that lamp; and What grieves me" most is, that I have been the cause of it. I was foolish enough to change the old lamp for a new one, and the next morning I found myself in this unknown country, which I am told is Africa."

"Princess," said Aladdin, interrupting her, "you have explained all by telling me we are in Africa. I desire you only to tell me if you know where the old lamp now is." "The African magician carries it carefully wrapt up in his bosom," said the princess; "and this I can assure you, because he pulled it out before me, and showed it to me in triumph."

"Princess," said Aladdin, "I think I have found the means to deliver you and to regain possession of the lamp, on which all my prosperity depends. To execute this design it is necessary for me to go to the town. I shall return by noon, and will then tell you what must be done by you to insure success. In the meantime I shall disguise myself; and I beg that the private door may be opened at the first knock."

When Aladdin was out of the palace, he looked around him on all sides, and perceiving a peasant going into the country, hastened after him; and when he had overtaken him, made a proposal to him to change clothes, which the man agreed to. When they had made the exchange, the countryman went about his business, and Aladdin entered the neighboring city. After traversing several streets, he came to that part of the town where the merchants and artisans had their particular streets according to their trades. He went into that of the druggists, and entering one of the largest and best furnished shops, asked the druggist if he had a certain powder, which he named.

The druggist, judging Aladdin by his habit to be very poor, told him he had it, but that it was very dear. Upon which Aladdin, penetrating his thoughts, pulled out his purse, and, showing him some gold, asked for half a dram of the powder, which the druggist weighed and gave him, telling him the price was a piece of gold. Aladdin put the money into his hand, and hastened to the palace, which he entered at once by the private door. When he came into the princess's apartment, he said to her, "Princess, you must take your part in the scheme which I propose for our deliverance.

You must overcome your aversion to the magician, and assume a most friendly manner toward him, and ask him to oblige you by partaking of an entertainment in your apartments. Before he leaves ask him to exchange cups with you, which he, gratified at the honor you do him, will gladly do, when you must give him the cup containing this powder. On drinking it he will instantly fall asleep, and we will obtain the lamp, whose slaves will do all our bidding, and restore us and the palace to the capital of China."

The princess obeyed to the utmost her husband's instructions. She assumed a look of pleasure on the next visit of the magician, and asked him to an entertainment, which he most willingly accepted. At the close of the evening, during which the princess had tried all she could to please him, she asked him to exchange cups with her, and, giving the signal, had the drugged cup brought to her, which she gave to the magician. He drank it out of compliment to the princess to the very last drop, when he fell backward lifeless on the sofa.

The princess, in anticipation of the success of her scheme, had so placed her women from the great hall to the foot of the staircase, that the word was no sooner given that the African magician was fallen backward, than the door was opened and Aladdin admitted to the hall. The princess rose from her seat, and ran overjoyed to embrace him; but he stopped her, and said, "Princess, retire to your apartment, and let me be left alone, while I endeavor to transport you back to China as speedily as you were brought from thence."

When the princess, her women, and slaves were gone out of the hall, Aladdin shut the door, and going directly to the dead body of the magician, opened his vest, took out the lamp, which was carefully wrapped up, and rubbing it, the genie immediately appeared. "Genie," said Aladdin, "I command thee to transport this palace instantly to the place from whence it was brought hither." The genie bowed his head in token of obedience, and disappeared. Immediately the palace was transported into China, and its removal was only felt by two little shocks, the one when it was lifted up, the other when it was set down, and both in a very short interval of time.

Aladdin Story part - 10

- Aladdin Story part - 10

On the morning after the restoration of Aladdin's palace, the sultan was looking out of his window, and mourning over the fate of his daughter, when he thought that he saw the vacancy created by the disappearance of the palace to be again filled up. On looking more attentively he was convinced beyond the power of doubt that it was his son-in-law's palace. Joy and gladness succeeded to sorrow and grief. He at once ordered a horse to be saddled, which he mounted that instant, thinking he could not make haste enough to the place.

Aladdin rose that morning by daybreak, put on one of the most magnificent habits his wardrobe afforded, and went up into the hall of twenty-four windows, from whence he perceived the sultan approaching, and received him at the foot of the great staircase, helping him to dismount.

He led the sultan into the princess's apartment. The happy father embraced her with tears of joy; and the princess, on her side, afforded similar testimonies of her extreme pleasure. After a short interval devoted to mutual explanations of all that had happened, the sultan restored Aladdin to his favor, and expressed his regret for the apparent harshness with which he had treated him.

"My son," said he, "be not displeased at my proceedings against you; they arose from my paternal love, and therefore you ought to forgive the excesses to which it hurried me." "Sire," replied Aladdin, "I have not the least reason to complain of your conduct, since you did nothing but what your duty required. This infamous magician, the basest of men, was the sole cause of my misfortune."

The African magician, who was thus twice foiled in his endeavor to ruin Aladdin, had a younger brother, who was as skilful a magician as himself, and exceeded him in wickedness and hatred of mankind. By mutual agreement they communicated with each other once a year, however widely separate might be their place of residence from each other. The younger brother, not having received as usual his annual communication, prepared to take a horoscope and ascertain his brother's proceedings. He, as well as his brother, always carried a geomantic square instrument about him; he prepared the sand, cast the points, and drew the figures. On examining the planetary crystal, he found that his brother was no longer living, but had been poisoned; and by another observation, that he was in the capital of the kingdom of China; also that the person who had poisoned him was of mean birth, though married to a princess, a sultan's daughter.

When the magician had informed himself of his brother's fate, he resolved immediately to avenge his death, and at once departed for China; where, after crossing plains, rivers, mountains, deserts, and a long tract of country without delay, he arrived after incredible fatigues. When he came to the capital of China, he took a lodging at a khan. His magic art soon revealed to him that Aladdin was the person who had been the cause of the death of his brother. He had heard, too, all the persons of repute in the city talking of a woman called Fatima, who was retired from the world, and of the miracles she wrought. As he fancied that this woman might be serviceable to him in the project he had conceived, he made more minute inquiries, and requested to be informed more particularly who that holy woman was, and what sort of miracles she performed.

"What!" said the person whom he addressed, "have you never seen or heard of her? She is the admiration of the whole town, for her fasting, her austerities, and her exemplary life. Except Mondays and Fridays, she never stirs out of her little cell; and on those days on which she comes into the town she does an infinite deal of good; for there is not a person who is diseased but she puts her hand on them and cures them."

Having ascertained the place where the hermitage of the holy woman was, the magician went at night, and, plunging a poniard into her heartâ€"killed this good woman. In the morning he dyed his face of the same hue as hers, and arraying himself in her garb, taking her veil, the large necklace she wore round her waist, and her stick, went straight to the palace of Aladdin.

As soon as the people saw the holy woman, as they imagined him to be, they presently gathered about him in a great crowd. Some begged his blessing, some kissed his hand, and others, more reserved, only the hem of his garment; while others, suffering from disease, stooped for him to lay his hands upon them, which he did, muttering some words in form of prayer, and, in short, counterfeiting so well that everybody took him for the holy woman. He came at last to the square before Aladdin's palace. The crowd and the noise was so great that the princess, who was in the hall of four-and-twenty windows, heard it, and asked what was the matter. One of her women told her it was a great crowd of people collected about the holy woman to be cured of diseases by the imposition of her hands.

The princess, who had long heard of this holy woman, but had never seen her, was very desirous to have some conversation with her; which the chief officer perceiving, told her it was an easy matter to bring her to her, if she desired and commanded it; and the princess, expressing her wishes, he immediately sent four slaves for the pretended holy woman.

As soon as the crowd saw the attendants from the palace, they made way; and the magician, perceiving also that they were coming for him, advanced to meet them, overjoyed to find his plot succeed so well. "Holy woman," said one of the slaves, "the princess wants to see you, and has sent us for you." "The princess does me too great an honor," replied the false Fatima; "I am ready to obey her command," and at the same time followed the slaves to the palace.

When the pretended Fatima had made her obeisance, the princess said, "My good mother, I have one thing to request, which you must not refuse me: it is, to stay with me, that you may edify me with your way of living, and that I may learn from your good example." "Princess," said the counterfeit Fatima, "I beg of you not to ask what I cannot consent to without neglecting my prayers and devotion." "That shall be no hindrance to you," answered the princess; "I have a great many apartments unoccupied; you shall choose which you like best, and have as much liberty to perform your devotions as if you were in your own cell."

The magician, who really desired nothing more than to introduce himself into the palace, where it would be a much easier matter for him to execute his designs, did not long excuse himself from accepting the obliging offer which the princess made him. "Princess," said he, "whatever resolution a poor wretched woman as I am may have made to renounce the pomp and grandeur of this world, I dare not presume to oppose the will and commands of so pious and charitable a princess."

Upon this the princess, rising up, said, "Come with me; I will show you what vacant apartments I have, that you may make choice of that you like best." The magician followed the princess, and of all the apartments she showed him made choice of that which was the worst, saying that it was too good for him, and that he only accepted it to please her.

Afterward, the princess would have brought him back again into the great hall to make him dine with her; but he, considering that he should then be obliged to show his face, which he had always taken care to conceal with Fatima's veil, and fearing that the princess should find out that he was not Fatima, begged of her earnestly to excuse him, telling her that he never ate anything but bread and dried fruits, and desiring to eat that slight repast in his own apartment. The princess granted his request, saying, "You may be as free here, good mother, as if you were in your own cell: I will order you a dinner, but remember I expect you as soon as you have finished your repast."

After the princess had dined, and the false Fatima had been sent for by one of the attendants, he again waited upon her.

"My good mother," said the princess, "I am overjoyed to see so holy a woman as yourself, who will confer a blessing upon this palace. But now I am speaking of the palace, pray how do you like it? And before I show it all to you, tell me first what you think of this hall."

Upon this question the counterfeit Fatima surveyed the hall from one end to the other. When he had examined it well, he said to the princess, "As far as such a solitary being as I am, who am unacquainted with what the world calls beautiful, can judge, this hall is truly admirable; there wants but one thing." "What is that, good mother?" demanded the princess; "tell me, I conjure you. For my part, I always believed, and have heard say, it wanted nothing; but if it does, it shall be supplied."

"Princess," said the false Fatima, with great dissimulation, "forgive me the liberty I have taken; but my opinion is, if it can be of any importance, that if a roc's egg were hung up in the middle of the dome, this hall would have no parallel in the four quarters of the world, and your palace would be the wonder of the universe."

"My good mother," said the princess, "what is a roc, and where may one get an egg?" "Princess," replied the pretended Fatima, "it is a bird of prodigious size, which inhabits the summit of Mount Caucasus; the architect who built your palace can get you one."

After the princess had thanked the false Fatima for what she believed her good advice, she conversed with her upon other matters; but could not forget the roc's egg, which she resolved to request of Aladdin when next he should visit her apartments. He did so in the course of that evening, and shortly after he entered, the princess thus addressed him: "I always believed that our palace was the most superb, magnificent, and complete in the world: but I will tell you now what it wants, and that is a roc's egg hung up in the midst of the dome." "Princess," replied Aladdin, "it is enough that you think it wants such an ornament; you shall see by the diligence which I use in obtaining it, that there is nothing which I would not do for your sake."

Aladdin left the Princess Buddir al Buddoor that moment, and went up into the hall of four-and-twenty windows, where, pulling out of his bosom the lamp, which after the danger he had been exposed to he always carried about him, he rubbed it; upon which the genie immediately appeared. "Genie," said Aladdin, "I command thee in the name of this lamp, bring a roc's egg to be hung up in the middle of the dome of the hall of the palace."

Aladdin had no sooner pronounced these words than the hall shook as if ready to fall; and the genie said in a loud and terrible voice, "Is it not enough that I and the other slaves of the lamp have done everything for you, but you, by an unheard of ingratitude, must command me to bring my master, and hang him up in the midst of this dome? This attempt deserves that you, the princess, and the palace, should be immediately reduced to ashes; but you are spared because this request does not come from yourself. Its true author is the brother of the African magician, your enemy, whom you have destroyed. He is now in your palace, disguised in the habit of the holy woman Fatima, whom he has murdered; at his suggestion your wife makes this pernicious demand. His design is to kill you, therefore take care of yourself." After these words the genie disappeared.

Aladdin resolved at once what to do. He returned to the princess's apartment, and, without mentioning a word of what had happened, sat down, and complained of a great pain which had suddenly seized his head. On hearing this the princess told him how she had invited the holy Fatima to stay with her, and that she was now in the palace; and at the request of the prince, ordered her to be summoned to her at once.

When the pretended Fatima came, Aladdin said, "Come hither, good mother; I am glad to see you here at so fortunate a time. I am tormented with a violent pain in my head, and request your assistance, and hope you will not refuse me that cure which you impart to afflicted persons."

So saying, he rose, but held down his head. The counterfeit Fatima advanced toward him, with his hand all the time on a dagger concealed in his girdle under his gown; which Aladdin observing, he snatched the weapon from his hand, pierced him to the heart with his own dagger, and then pushed him down on the floor.

"My dear prince, what have you done?" cried the princess in surprise. "You have killed the holy woman!" "No, my princess," answered Aladdin with emotion, "I have not killed Fatima, but a villain, who would have assassinated me if I had not prevented him. This wicked man," added he, uncovering his face, "is the brother of the magician who attempted our ruin. He has strangled the true Fatima, and disguised himself in her clothes with intent to murder me."

Aladdin then informed her how the genie had told him these facts, and how narrowly she and the palace had escaped destruction through his treacherous suggestion which had led to her request.

Thus was Aladdin delivered from the persecution of the two brothers, who were magicians. Within a few years afterward the sultan died in a good old age, and as he left no male children, the Princess Buddir al Buddoor succeeded him, and she and Aladdin reigned together many years, and left a numerous and illustrious posterity.

CHAPTER TWO

Ch : 2 Ali Baba and Forty Thieves

- Ch : 2 Ali Baba and Forty Thieves

The story takes place in Baghdad during the Abbasid era. Ali Baba and his elder brother Cassim are the sons of Ali Baba and forty thievesa merchant. After the death of their father, the greedy Cassim marries a wealthy woman and becomes well-to-do, building on their father's business - but Ali Baba marries a poor woman and settles into the trade of a woodcutter.

One day Ali Baba is at work collecting and cutting firewood in the forest, and he happens to overhear a group of forty thieves visiting their treasure store. The treasure is in a cave, the mouth of which is sealed by magic. It opens on the words "Open, Simsim", and seals itself on the words "Close, Simsim". When the thieves are gone, Ali Baba enters the cave himself, and takes some of the treasure home.

Ali Baba borrows his sister-in-law's scales to weigh this new wealth of gold coins. Unbeknownst to Ali, she puts a blob of wax in the scales to find out what Ali is using them for, as she is curious to know what kind of grain her impoverished brother-in-law needs to measure. To her shock, she finds a gold coin sticking to the scales and tells her husband, Ali Baba's rich and greedy brother, Cassim. Under pressure from his brother, Ali Baba is forced to reveal the secret of the cave.

Cassim goes to the cave and enters with the magic words, but in his greed and excitement over the treasures forgets the magic words to get back out again. The thieves find him there, and kill him. When his brother does not come back, Ali Baba goes to the cave to look for him, and finds the body, quartered and with each piece displayed just inside the entrance of the cave to discourage any similar attempts in the future.

Ali Baba brings the body home, where he entrusts Morgiana, a clever slave-girl in Cassim's household, with the task of making others believe that Cassim has died a natural death. First, Morgiana purchases medicines from an apothecary, telling him that Cassim is gravely ill. Then, she finds an old tailor known as Baba Mustafa whom she pays, blindfolds, and leads to Cassim's house. There, overnight, the tailor stitches the pieces of Cassims' body back together, so that no one will be suspicious. Ali and his family are able to give Cassim a proper burial without anyone asking awkward questions.

The thieves, finding the body gone, realize that yet another person must know their secret, and set out to track him down. One of the thieves goes down to the town and comes across Baba Mustafa, who mentions that he has just sewn a dead man's body back together. Realizing that the dead man must have been the thieves' victim, the thief asks Baba Mustafa to lead the way to the house where the deed was performed. The tailor is blindfolded again, and in this state he is able to retrace his steps and find the house. The thief marks forty thieves the door with a symbol.

The plan is for the other thieves to come back that night and kill everyone in the house. However, the thief has been seen by Morgiana and she, loyal to her master, foils his plan by marking all the houses in the neighborhood with a similar marking. When the 40 thieves return that night, they cannot identify the correct house and the head thief kills the lesser thief.

The next day, another thief revisits Baba Mustafa and tries again, only this time, a chunk is chipped out of the stone step at Ali Baba's front door. Again Morgiana foils the plan by making similar chips in all the other doorsteps. The second thief is killed for his stupidity as well. At last, the head thief goes and looks for himself. This time, he memorizes every detail he can of the exterior of Ali Baba's house.

The chief of the thieves pretends to be an oil merchant in need of Ali Baba's hospitality, bringing with him Forty thieves hiding in oil jarsmules loaded with thirty-eight oil jars, one filled with oil, the other thirty-seven hiding the other remaining thieves. Once Ali Baba is asleep, the thieves plan to kill him. Again, Morgiana discovers and foils the plan, killing the thirty-seven thieves in their oil jars by pouring boiling oil on them. When their leader comes to rouse his men, he discovers that they are dead, and escapes.

To exact revenge, after some time the thief establishes himself as a merchant, befriends Ali Baba's son (who is now in charge of the late Cassim's business), and is invited to dinner at Ali Baba's house. The thief is recognized by Morgiana, who performs a dance with a dagger for the diners and plunges it into the heart of the thief when he is off his guard.

Ali Baba is at first angry with Morgiana, but when he finds out the thief tried to kill him, he gives Morgiana her freedom and marries her to his son. Ali Baba is then left as the only one knowing the secret of the treasure in the cave and how to access it. Thus, the story ends happily for everyone except the forty thieves and Cassim.

Thank You So Much Message

For Your Supported & For Your Loves Thank You So Much. Have A Greatest Day Of Your. If I am successful today, because of my father, if he lived today, he would have been very happy, he will always and always be with me.